JOY TO THE WORLD

CHRISTMAS STORIES AND SONGS

TOMIE dePAOLA

JOY TO THE WORLD

CHRISTMAS STORIES AND SONGS

G. P. PUTNAM'S SONS
AN IMPRINT OF PENGUIN GROUP (USA) INC.

G. P. PUTNAM'S SONS

A division of Penguin Young Readers Group.
Published by The Penguin Group.
Penguin Group (USA) Inc., 375 Hudson Street, New York, NY 10014, U.S.A.
Penguin Group (Canada), 90 Eglinton Avenue East, Suite 700, Toronto, Ontario M4P 2Y3, Canada (a division of Pearson Penguin Canada Inc.).
Penguin Books Ltd, 80 Strand, London WC2R 0RL, England.
Penguin Ireland, 25 St. Stephen's Green, Dublin 2, Ireland (a division of Penguin Books Ltd.).
Penguin Group (Australia), 250 Camberwell Road, Camberwell, Victoria 3124, Australia (a division of Pearson Australia Group Pty Ltd).
Penguin Books India Pvt Ltd, 11 Community Centre, Panchsheel Park, New Delhi - 110 017, India.
Penguin Group (NZ), 67 Apollo Drive, Rosedale, North Shore 0632, New Zealand (a division of Pearson New Zealand Ltd).
Penguin Books (South Africa) (Pty) Ltd, 24 Sturdee Avenue, Rosebank, Johannesburg 2196, South Africa.
Penguin Books Ltd, Registered Offices: 80 Strand, London WC2R 0RL, England.

Library of Congress Cataloging-in-Publication Data is available upon request.

ISBN 978-0-399-25536-6
1 3 5 7 9 10 8 6 4 2

Contents

O Little Town of Bethlehem

Phillips Brooks, 1868

Lewis H. Redner, 1868

3. How silently, how silently,
   The wondrous gift is given!
   So God imparts to human hearts
   The blessings of His heaven.
   No ear may hear His coming;
   But in this world of sin,
   Where meek souls will receive Him, still
   The dear Christ enters in.

4. O holy Child of Bethlehem,
   Descend to us, we pray;
   Cast out our sin, and enter in;
   Be born in us today.
   We hear the Christmas angels
   The great glad tidings tell;
   O come to us, abide with us,
   Our Lord Emmanuel.

THE Night OF Las Posadas

TOMIE dePAOLA

For my New London friends, Fr. Dick Lower
and the parishioners of Our Lady of Fatima Church,
who were the first ones to hear this story;
for my Santa Fe friends, Alice Ann, Malcolm,
Christine, Davis, Susan, Jim, Ivan, and Allison;
for my L.A. friend, Roberto,
and most importantly, for my Mexican friend, Mario

GLOSSARY

Farolitos • lanterns made of candles in paper bags

Luminarias • bonfires that light the way

Posada • inn

Santero maker • a wood carver who makes images of saints

Tía • aunt

Turistas • tourists

A NOTE FROM THE AUTHOR

Las Posadas, an old Spanish custom that celebrates Mary and Joseph seeking shelter
in Bethlehem on Christmas Eve, stems from the word *posada*, meaning "inn." It began in
Spain and came to the New World, first to Mexico and then to the American Southwest.

In Spain and Mexico, Las Posadas is celebrated for nine days. Families walk in
procession, knocking on doors, but only on Christmas Eve does a door open. Everyone enters and has hot chocolate and cookies to commemorate the expected birth of
the Holy Child.

In San Antonio, Texas, a procession of boats winds down the river that runs
through the center of the city, with the couple representing Mary and Joseph sitting in
the first boat, followed by boats filled with people singing.

In Santa Fe, New Mexico, where I have imagined my story, *luminaries* or *farolitos*,
as they are called in New Mexico, line the edges of the Plaza in the historical district of
the city. These candles placed in paper bags light the way for Mary and Joseph, the
procession of candle bearers, and others singing traditional Spanish songs. The procession
is usually made up of people from Santa Cruz, a small village north of the city. It is a
great honor to be chosen to play Mary and Joseph. Along the way, Mary and Joseph
knock on doors, five in all. A song is sung each time, asking for them to be let in, and a
"devil" appears with an answering song to keep them out of the "inn." It is very dramatic
and even amusing as the crowds of people filling the square boo and hiss at the devil.
The procession moves around the Plaza until it reaches the Palace of the Governors.
There, the gates are thrown open to a courtyard where, as in Spain and Mexico, hot
chocolate and cookies are served, and everyone celebrates the coming of the baby Jesus.

—TdeP

In a little village high in the mountains above Santa Fe, preparations for Las Posadas had been going on for weeks.

Sister Angie was so proud. Her niece, Lupe, and Lupe's new husband, Roberto, had been chosen to portray Maria and José—Mary and Joseph.

Sister Angie had been in charge of Las Posadas for years and years. It was she who trained the singers who followed Maria and José as they made their way around the Plaza in old Santa Fe and finally into the courtyard of the Palace of Governors, where an empty manger waited for the birth of the Holy Child.

"Now," Sister Angie said, speaking to the two men who would play the devils, "here's a picture of what your faces are going to look like." She wanted to make sure they knew how to paint their faces with black eyebrows and beards, and that their red satin costumes were just right, especially the red capes and head caps with pointy red horns. The Devil would snarl and hiss as he tried to keep Maria and José from finding shelter. (The Plaza was so big that two devils were needed to rush from balcony to balcony without being seen by the crowd.)

Sister Angie always made the costumes for Maria and José herself. Blue and white for Maria, brown for José.

"Stand still," she told Roberto. "Lupe, I hope he isn't as fidgety at home."

"Oh, no, Tía Angie. He's just nervous about being José."

"Ah, well," Sister Angie said. "Let's just go to the church and look at Maria and José. They will give you inspiration, Roberto."

Miguel Ovideo, the *Santero* maker, had made a beautiful carving of Maria and José for the Golden Jubilee of Sister Angie the year before. Fifty years as a sister. Father Vasquez had put the carving in a place of honor in the church. As Christmas drew near, it was moved near the altar rail.

They stood looking up at Maria and José on their way to Bethlehem. "Just think of the carving and try to look like them," Sister Angie told them.

"I will," promised Roberto. "At least we don't have to worry about a burro."

Las Posadas didn't have a burro in the procession. Maria and José walked. The burro had only made problems, so they had stopped using one years ago.

Finally it was the night of Las Posadas. And Sister Angie came down with the flu.

"There is no way you can go tonight," the doctor told her. "Walking in all that cold weather—and they say that snow is coming. They will just have to get along without you this year." For the first time, Sister Angie would not be at Las Posadas.

"Don't worry, *Tía*," Lupe told her. "We will make you proud this evening."

In the streets leading to the Plaza, men were busy putting the *farolitos* in place. They would be lit as soon as it got dark.

Wood for the bonfire was stacked in the courtyard just off the Plaza, ready to be set ablaze when Maria and José entered.

"Well," one of the men said, "it looks as if it will be a white Christmas. Snow is on the way." Even as he spoke, flakes drifted down. "But a little snow never stops Las Posadas."

Up in the village, the singers, the candlebearers—and the devils—
piled into their cars. They wanted to get down the mountain before
the snow, which was beginning to fall heavily. "Do you have
the music?" "Where's my guitar?" "Wait, I forgot my gloves and
earmuffs." "I'm so nervous." "It's a good thing you're not Maria.
You'd faint." "Mi, mi, mi." "I hope my voice is loud enough. I've
never sung the Devil before." It was the same every year.

Sister Angie looked out of her window. Yes, she wiped away a tear as she saw Roberto's old pickup pull up outside. Lupe and Roberto got out and rang the doorbell. They wanted Sister Angie to see them in their costumes.

"Ah, Maria and José. You look wonderful. If I had my way, I'd offer you shelter right here! Now, give me a kiss and be off."

Roberto and Lupe were the last to leave the village. Roberto's pickup had been acting up lately, and the deep snow didn't help. A sudden skid and the motor died. What to do?

"I'll walk ahead to see if I can get some help," Roberto told Lupe. "Wrap up and I'll be back before you know it."

Down in the town, everyone had gathered. The snow had tapered off and was falling gently. The *farolitos* were lit. The Plaza looked magical.

"Where are Lupe and Roberto?" Father Vasquez asked. "It's almost time to start."

The guitars were tuned, the horn player had warmed up, the singers were ready. Even the devils were ready. But no Roberto and Lupe. And everyone knows that you can't have Las Posadas without Maria and José.

Suddenly, down the street came a young couple. The man was leading a burro, carrying a young woman.

"We are friends of Sister Angie," the man said. "Roberto and Lupe are stuck in the snow on the mountain road, so we have come to take their place. We know what to do, and we thought our burro could be in the procession, too. My wife is going to have a baby and it would be better for her to ride."

"Let's go then," Father Vasquez said gratefully.

The candlebearers led the way, followed by Maria and José. The musicians followed and then came the singers. Out into the Plaza they went. Everyone knew their part, even the burro.

They stopped at the first door. "Oh, let the holy couple in—give them shelter—let Maria rest so that the Holy Child can be born," they sang.

José knocked with his staff. Maria looked down from the burro and smiled sweetly.

But the Devil appeared. "NO! NO! Don't let them in," he sang out. "Look at them—how poor, how wretched! They have no money." The crowd booed and shouted.

The procession moved on, knocking on one door after another. Sometimes the Devil popped out at them, and the crowd booed even louder. And sometimes they knocked, and no one answered.

It was one of the most beautiful Las Posadas ever held. Even the young woman playing Maria was about to be a mother just like the mother of the Holy Child. Perfect. They reached the gates to the courtyard. Once more they sang, asking to be let in.

This time no Devil. The gates opened wide.

The bonfire blazed, and everyone rushed in. A little pushing and shoving, but that was all right. Everyone wanted to be near the manger.

"Well, you certainly saved Las Posadas," Father Vasquez said, turning to thank the young couple who had taken Lupe and Roberto's place. But they were nowhere to be seen. Maybe they didn't know that they were to sit in the special place near the empty manger.

"Father Vasquez. We are so sorry to be late!" It was Lupe and Roberto, calling out as they rushed into the courtyard. "Did we ruin everything?"

"No, no," Father Vasquez said. "Sister Angie's friends were here. They led the procession, but now I can't find them. Go quickly and sit by the manger."

"What friends?" Lupe whispered to Roberto.

Sister Angie woke with a start. Las Posadas would be over. Everyone would be having their hot chocolate and cookies. The villagers would be back in an hour or two. I hope Lupe and Roberto did well, she thought.

Sister Angie was feeling so much better. She looked out of the window. The snow had almost stopped. Drifts covered the rooftops and the street below.

"I'll just go over to the church and light a candle," she said to herself. She bundled up and put the key to the church in her pocket.

Sister Angie crossed the street and stood in front of the church. Footprints in the snow on the steps led up to the door. She didn't think too much of it. Maybe some *turistas*—they came at all hours expecting the church to be open.

Inside, the church was dark except for the candle burning in front of the Blessed Sacrament. "I'll light a candle in front of the carving," she said. She took an unlit candle and struck a match. The candle flared up and settled into a steady glow.

Sister Angie knelt down and placed her candle in front of the carving. "Oh, Maria. Oh, José," she prayed, eyes closed, "my heart will always be open to you so that the Holy Child will have a place to be born."

Sister Angie opened her eyes. There, in front of her, she saw
wet footprints leading to the carving. She looked up.

The cloaks of Maria and José were covered in fresh snow.

Silent Night

Joseph Möhr, 1818

Franz Grüber, 1818

Tenderly

1. Si - lent night! Ho - ly night! All is calm, all is bright.
2. Si - lent night! Ho - ly night! Shep - herds quake at the sight!
3. Si - lent night! Ho - ly night! Son of God, love's pure light!

'Round yon vir - gin moth - er and child! Ho - ly In - fant, so ten - der and mild,
Glo - ries stream_ from heav - en a - far, Heav'n-ly hosts_ sing, "Al - le - lu - ia!"
Ra - diant beams_ from Thy ho-ly face, With the dawn of re - deem - ing grace,

Sleep in heav - en-ly peace,_ Sleep_ in heav - en - ly peace._
Christ, the Sav - ior, is born!_ Christ,_ the Sav - ior, is born!_
Je - sus, Lord at Thy birth,_ Je sus, Lord at Thy birth._

The First Noël

Traditional

16th century French

Moderately

1. The__ first___ No - ël the__ an - gels did say Was to
2. They__ look - èd___ up and__ saw___ a star Shin - ing

cer - tain poor shep - herds in fields as they lay; In__ fields__ where they lay__
in___ the east___ be - yond__ them far, And__ to___ the__ earth it__

keep - ing their sheep On a cold win -ter's night___ that was___ so deep.
gave___ great light, And___ so it con - tin -ued both day___ and night.

Refrain

No - ël,___ No - ël, No - ël, No - ël,___ Born is the King of Is - ra - el.

The Story of the
THREE WISE KINGS

Retold & illustrated by

TOMIE dePAOLA

To FLORENCE ALEXANDER,
a wonderful lady, a superb agent
and a very dear friend

A Word about the Kings

The first written word about the kings appears in the Gospel of St. Matthew. His brief account tells of wise men who went to Bethlehem to honor the child who would become King of the Jews. Matthew does not give them names nor does he say how many wise men there were. His only mention as to where they came from is that they followed a star from the East.

Over the centuries details about the wise men were added gradually. In the second century, they were transformed into kings and their number was determined. Early art from the period shows two and four figures, but three figures were used most often and persisted into later centuries because Matthew had referred to three gifts.

By the eighth century, each of the kings had a name, an area from which he came, and physical descriptions. Melchior of Arabia was depicted as an old man; Gaspar of Tharsis as young; and Balthazar of Saba was shown as mature and black.

The feast of the three kings, called the Feast of the Epiphany, is celebrated on January 6th, twelve days after Christmas. In some countries, this is the day on which gifts are given.

In this book, I have chosen to paint the mother and child in the traditional pose referred to as "Seat of Wisdom, Throne of Justice." This pose was frequently used in Romanesque paintings of the Adoration of the Kings.

TdeP   1983

Long ago in the East,
in lands far from one another,
there lived three kings—
Melchior of Arabia,
Gaspar of Tharsis,
and Balthazar of Saba.

These wise men studied the stars.

Each night,
they looked at the sky
and wrote down where the stars were,
where they had come from,
and where they were going.

51

One night,
a star they had never seen before
appeared in the sky.

Each of the kings consulted his books
and found that this new star was the sign
that a great king was about to be born.

So each king, not knowing about the others,
set out to follow the star,
to find the child-king
and to honor him.

And each carried with him a gift.
Melchior took gold;
Gaspar, frankincense;
and Balthazar, myrrh.

After many days and nights,
the three wise kings met.
They found that they were all following the same star
so they continued their journey together.

But as they came near to Jerusalem,
they lost sight of the star
and they did not know which way to go.

"Let us ask at the palace of King Herod,"
one of them said.
"Surely Herod will know of the birth
of another great king."

"Where is he that has been born
to be king of the Jews?" they asked.
"We have seen his star in the East
and we have come to honor him."

Now Herod, who was an evil man,
was disturbed when he heard this.
He wished to be
the only king in that land.
He went to his chief priests and learned men
and asked them where this child would be born.

"It has been written:
at Bethlehem in Judah,"
they told him.

Herod sent for the three kings.
"Go to Bethlehem
and find out all about the child-king,"
he said.
"And when you have found him,
come back and tell me
so I may worship him too."

The three wise kings
set out for Bethlehem
not knowing that Herod wanted to destroy
the newborn baby.
And there in the sky,
once again, was the star.

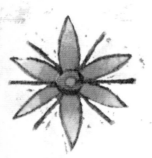

They followed it
until it stopped over the place
where the child was born.

Like a flame of fire
that star pointed out God,
the King of Kings.

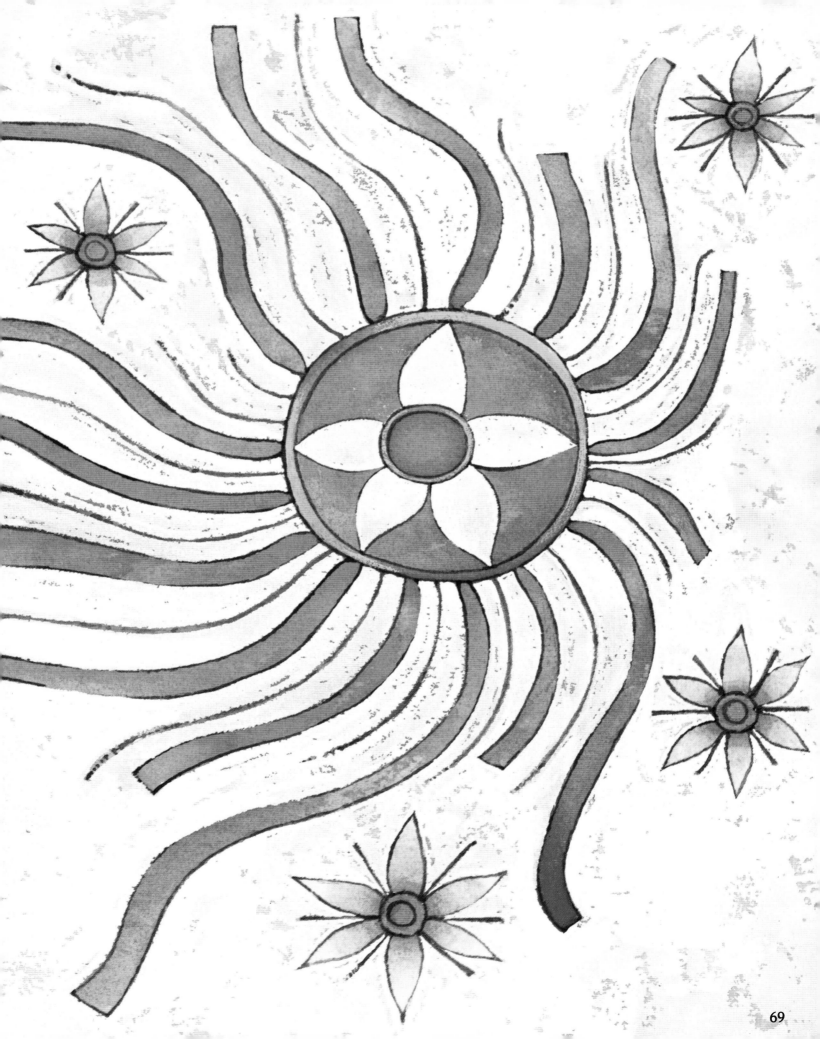

And going into the place,
they saw the child with his mother, Mary,
and falling down on their knees they honored him.
Then, they opened their treasures
and offered the gifts
of gold and frankincense and myrrh.

That night as the kings slept,
they were warned in a dream
not to go back to Herod,
for he wished to destroy the child.

So the three kings,
to keep Herod from finding the child,
returned to their countries
by a different way.

Away in a Manger

Anonymous

15th century German
Arranged by Nick Nicholson

Softly

1. A - way in a man - ger, no crib for a bed, The
2. The cat - tle are low - ing, the poor ba - by wakes, But

lit - tle Lord Je - sus laid down His sweet head, The
lit - tle Lord Je - sus, no cry - ing He makes, I

stars in the sky, ____ looked down where He lay, The
love Thee, Lord Je - sus, look down from the sky, And

lit - tle Lord Je - sus, a - sleep on the hay.
stay by my cra - dle, till morn - ing is nigh.

The Legend of
the Poinsettia

retold and illustrated by
Tomie dePaola

To Chris O'Brien, who knows
that the beauty of the gift is in the giving.

Author's Note

When I first heard the Mexican legend of the poinsettia, about a little girl who offers weeds to the Christ Child as her gift for Christmas, I was touched by it as only Christmas can touch me. I knew that one day I wanted to create the story in pictures for children.

This lovely Mexican wildflower is known by many names in Mexico: *flor de fuego* (fire flower), *flor de Navidad* (Christmas flower), and *flor de la Nochebuena* (flower of the Holy Night), the name I have used in my story.

The poinsettia found its way to the United States through Dr. Joel Roberts Poinsett, who served as our nation's minister to Mexico from 1825 to 1830. He was fascinated with its beauty and called the plant "painted leaves," because the part often thought of as the flower actually consists of leaves surrounding a smaller flower portion. He took cuttings home with him to South Carolina when he returned from Mexico in 1830.

The Christmas plant, which we call poinsettia after Dr. Poinsett, found its way into our own Christmas traditions, and nothing seems to say "Merry Christmas" better than a beautiful red and green poinsettia. TdeP

Lucida lived in a small village
high up in the mountains of Mexico
with her mama, her papa,
and her younger brother and sister, Paco and Lupe.
Papa worked in the fields with their burro, Pepito.
Every evening Lucida fed Pepito, gave him fresh water,
and filled his stall with clean straw.

At home Lucida helped Mama
clean their *casita*—their little house—
and pat out the tortillas for their meals.

She took care of Paco and Lupe, and each evening
they went to the shrine of the Virgin of Guadalupe
near the front gate to see if fresh candles were needed.

But every day was not work.
On Sundays the family went to San Gabriel
in the square where Padre Alvarez said the Mass.
And all through the year there were fiestas
and holy days, which always began with a procession
that wound through the village and ended in San Gabriel.

One day, close to Christmas—*la Navidad*—
Padre Alvarez came to their casita.
"Ah, Señora Martinez, *buenos días*—good day,"
Padre Alvarez said. "I am here to ask you about the blanket
which covers the figure of the Baby Jesus
in the Christmas procession.

We have used the same one for so many years
that it is almost worn out.
Because your weaving is so fine, I have come to ask
if you would make a new one."
"*Mi padre*," Lucida's mother said, "I would be honored.
And Lucida will help me."

On Saturday Lucida and Mama went to the market
to buy the wool for the blanket. They chose
the finest yarn they could find.

At home Lucida helped Mama dye the wool
the colors of the rainbow.
"Those colors will shine throughout the church,"
Papa said, as he watched Lucida and Mama
string the yarn on the loom.

As Christmas drew closer,
everyone in the village was busy.
All the mamas were making gifts to place
at the manger of the Baby Jesus in the church.
The papas worked together putting up
the manger scene in San Gabriel.

Lucida and the other children went to the church
for singing practice for the Christmas Eve procession,
when everyone would walk to San Gabriel,
singing and carrying candles.
Once inside, Padre Alvarez would lay
the figure of the Baby Jesus in the manger,
and the villagers would go up
and place their gifts around it.
"Our gift will be the blanket for the Baby Jesus,"
Lucida told her friends. "I am helping Mama weave it."

One afternoon a few days before Christmas Eve,
Lucida and the children were singing in the church
when Señora Gomez came hurrying in.
"Lucida, you must come home. Your mama is sick
and your papa has taken her down to the town
to see the doctor. You must take care of your
brother and sister until your papa returns tonight."
Lucida was frightened. Mama had never been sick before.

When she got home, Paco and Lupe were crying.
They were frightened, too. Lucida tried to comfort them.
She made some food and sat down to wait for Papa.

That evening Papa came in looking tired and worried.
He drew Lucida close and said, "Lucida, *mi niña,*
your mama is ill. Your aunt—Tía Carmen—
will take care of Mama until she is well,
but I must go back and stay with Mama
until I can bring her home.
But it won't be until after Christmas.
Señora Gomez will take care of you and Paco and Lupe
while I am gone. She will come for you tomorrow."

The next afternoon Lucida overheard two women talking.
"Lucida's mama is ill. She won't be able to finish
the blanket for the procession. Isn't it a shame?"
"*Sí*," the other woman said. "We are all so disappointed.
Padre Alvarez will have to use the old worn-out one."

When Lucida went home to feed Pepito
and get clothes for Paco, Lupe, and herself,
she looked at the unfinished blanket on the loom.

Perhaps I can finish it, she thought.
But when she sat down and tried to weave,
the yarn got tangled. The more she tried
to untangle it, the worse it got. It was no use.
She could never finish it by herself.

She took the unfinished blanket to Señora Gomez.
"Oh, Lucida, it is so tangled. There isn't time
for me to fix it," Señora Gomez told her.
"Tomorrow is Christmas Eve."
Lucida started to cry.
It was her fault the blanket was ruined.

Her family wouldn't have a gift
to place at the manger of the Baby Jesus.
"Don't worry, Lucida. We will all go
to the procession together."
Lucida didn't say anything, but in her heart
she felt that she had ruined Christmas.

"Come, Paco; come, Lupe. It is time to go to the procession," Señora Gomez called on Christmas Eve. "Where is Lucida?" She was nowhere to be found. Lucida was hiding.

From the shadows, Lucida watched everyone gather
for the procession. The candles were lit, the singing began,
and the villagers walked to San Gabriel,
carrying gifts to place at the manger.
Lucida walked along in the darkness
and watched the procession go into the church,
followed by Padre Alvarez carrying the Baby Jesus.

"Little girl, are you Lucida?" An old woman
  stood in the shadows nearby.
"*Sí*," Lucida answered, wondering who she was.
"I have a message for you. Your mama is going to be fine,
  and your papa will bring her home soon.
So you don't have to worry.
Go now into the church and celebrate Christmas
  with the others. Paco and Lupe are waiting for you."

"I can't," Lucida told her. "I don't have a gift
  for the Baby Jesus.
  Mama and I were weaving a beautiful blanket,
  but I couldn't finish it.
  I tried, but I only tangled it all up."
"Ah, Lucida, any gift is beautiful because it is given,"
  the old woman told her. "Whatever you give, the Baby Jesus
  will love, because it comes from you."
"But what can I give now?" Lucida said, looking around.

A patch of tall green weeds grew in a tangle nearby.
Lucida rushed over and picked an armful.
"Do you think these will be all right?" Lucida turned
to ask the old woman, but she was gone.

Lucida walked into the church. It was blazing
with candlelight, and the children were singing
as she walked quietly down the aisle
with a bundle of green weeds in her arms.

"What is Lucida carrying?" a woman whispered.
"Why is she bringing weeds into the church?"
    another one murmured.
    Lucida reached the manger scene. She placed the green weeds
    around the stable. Then she lowered her head and prayed.

A hush fell over the church. Voices began to whisper.
"Look! Look at the weeds!"
Lucida opened her eyes and looked up.

Each weed was tipped with a flaming red star.
The manger glowed and shimmered
as if lit by a hundred candles.

When everyone went outside after the Mass,
all the clumps of tall green weeds
throughout the town were shining with red stars.
Lucida's simple gift had indeed become beautiful.

And every Christmas to this day, the red stars shine
on top of green branches in Mexico. The people
call the plants *la Flor de Nochebuena*—
the Flower of the Holy Night—the poinsettia.

Joy to the World!

Isaac Watts, 1719

George F. Handel, 1742
Arranged by Lowell Mason, 1830